RHODE ISLAND ROY

The Roughest Rooster in the World

WANTED

$100 Reward

Rose Impey G588
Shoo Rayner

ORCHARD BOOKS

ORCHARD BOOKS
96 Leonard Street, London EC2A 4RH
Orchard Books Australia
14 Mars Road, Lane Cove NSW 2066
First published in Great Britain 1995
First paperback publication 1995
Text © Rose Impey 1995
Illustrations © Shoo Rayner 1995
The right of Rose Impey to be identified as the author
and Shoo Rayner as the illustrator of this work has
been asserted by them in accordance with the
Copyright, Designs and Patents Act, 1988.
A CIP catalogue record for this book
is available from the British Library.
Hardback 1 85213 764 9
Paperback 1 85213 768 1
Printed in Great Britain

RHODE ISLAND ROY

Roy, the Rhode Island Rooster,
was the terror of the town.
He was big,
he was bad
and he was ugly.
Roy was the roughest rooster
in the world.

When Roy came into town,
all the kids were kept at home.
All the layabouts laid low.
All the bullies backed off.
Even the sheriff shut up shop.

In seconds the streets were clear
— except for Roy, of course.
He had the place to himself.
It was always the same.

As soon as Roy was hatched
you could see he was different.

He was, by far,
the ugliest fowl in town.
Roy couldn't help it,
but it was true.

All the other birds picked on him.
"Boy, are you ugly!" they said.

Everyone was rude to him
and pushed him around.
So Roy learned to fight first
and talk later.

Soon Roy had a reputation.

Everyone knew that Roy
had killed a couple of cats

and damaged a dog.

It was *said* that Roy
had head-butted a horse

and kidnapped a cow

and gunned down a goat.

Someone said that Roy
had wrestled with a rhino.
(They *said* they had seen him).

And tangled with a tiger.
(He had the scars to prove it).

The stories got worse and worse.
So nobody stayed around,
when Roy came to town.

Roy strutted into the saloon.
"Give me a drink," he said.
"And make it snappy."
He leaned back in his chair
with his feet on the table
and looked as mean
and bad-tempered
as he knew how.

It wasn't easy.
Every time a big-headed bantam
or some turkeys, looking for trouble,
came to town
they soon heard about Roy.
They were never happy
until they'd picked a fight.

17

Roy knew they were only
looking for trouble
but what could he do?
Roy couldn't run back to his ranch,

or hide behind his horse,

or beg them to leave him alone.

Roy had his reputation to keep up.

So Roy kept on fighting.

Roy had wrestled more roosters,

crowed over more cockerels,

beat more bantams,

and chased more chickens
out of town,
than you have had roast dinners.

He had even, I'm sorry to say,
drunk more turkeys under the table.
And won more bets to see
who could curse the worst.
By now, Roy was
a thoroughly bad lot.

Mothers told their children,
"You'd better be good,
or Roy the Rooster will get you."
Everyone was scared of him
so everyone kept well away.

But the fact was,
Roy was not a happy rooster.
His was a lonely life.
Roy was getting old.
He wanted to put up his feet
and take off his spurs.

He wanted to stop fighting
and go fishing.
He wanted a quiet life,
but he couldn't have it.
Not with a reputation to keep up.

Well, one day, a new family
came to town.
They were a very fine family.
They were American Leghorns.
There was a father, Louis,

and a mother, Lulu,

and their son Larry.

The Leghorns were very proud.
They kept themselves
to themselves.

They didn't hear about Roy.
They didn't know about
the roughest rooster in the world.

The next time Roy came to town,
the streets cleared as usual.
All the shops shut
and the cafés closed.
The whole town disappeared
and hid behind its curtains.
Except for the Leghorns.

The Leghorns didn't know
what was happening.
They were taking a morning walk
down the main street,
when Rhode Island Roy rode in.

Roy stopped his horse
in the middle of the street.
He looked at Mr Leghorn
and he looked at Mrs Leghorn
and he looked at Larry Leghorn.
And all the Leghorns looked back.
They'd never seen anyone so ugly
in the whole of their lives.

Mr Leghorn said nothing;
he knew trouble when he saw it.
Mrs Leghorn said nothing;
she was far too well-mannered.

But Larry was only a chick;
he saw no reason to be scared.
He was too young
to have learned about manners.

He stared and
he stared and
he stared.

Mr Leghorn gave a gasp.
Mrs Leghorn let out a long sigh.
The whole town,
peeping round its curtains,
held its breath.
You could have heard a feather dro

Softly, very softly,
there was the sound of crying.
Roy, the Rhode Island Rooster,
was sobbing like a baby.

The whole town was shocked.
No one had ever seen
a grown rooster cry before.
Everyone waited to see
what would happen.

Larry led Roy's horse
all the way down the street
to his house.

Roy, the roughest rooster
in the world,
took tea with the Leghorns.

He played games with Larry
until bedtime.

Then he read his new friend
a bedtime story.
It was about a foolish chicken,
called Licken,
who thought the sky had fallen in.

From that day on
Roy was a different character.

Now he had friends,
he could change his ways.
Now he could hang up his spurs,
put away his pistols
and retire from wrestling.

Roy became the most
respectable rooster in town.
And for the rest of his life
Roy was really happy,
which made him much less ugly.

CRACK-A-JOKE

Why did the turkey fall in love with the chicken?

Because she egged him on a bit!

Why did the turkey rush his dinner?

Because he was a little gobbler!

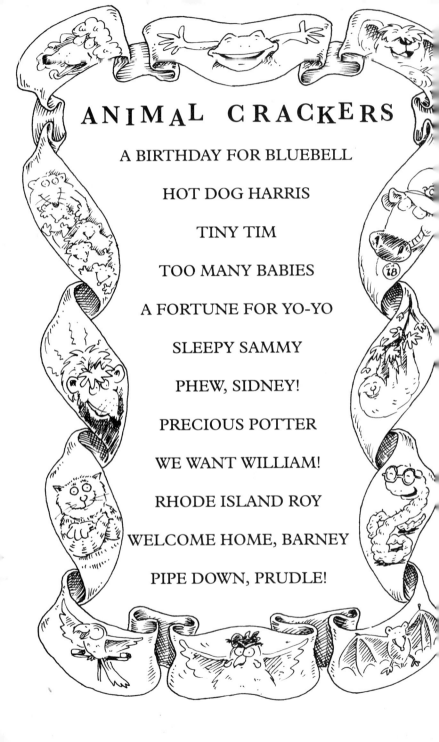

ANIMAL CRACKERS

A BIRTHDAY FOR BLUEBELL

HOT DOG HARRIS

TINY TIM

TOO MANY BABIES

A FORTUNE FOR YO-YO

SLEEPY SAMMY

PHEW, SIDNEY!

PRECIOUS POTTER

WE WANT WILLIAM!

RHODE ISLAND ROY

WELCOME HOME, BARNEY

PIPE DOWN, PRUDLE!